Vegetable Basket

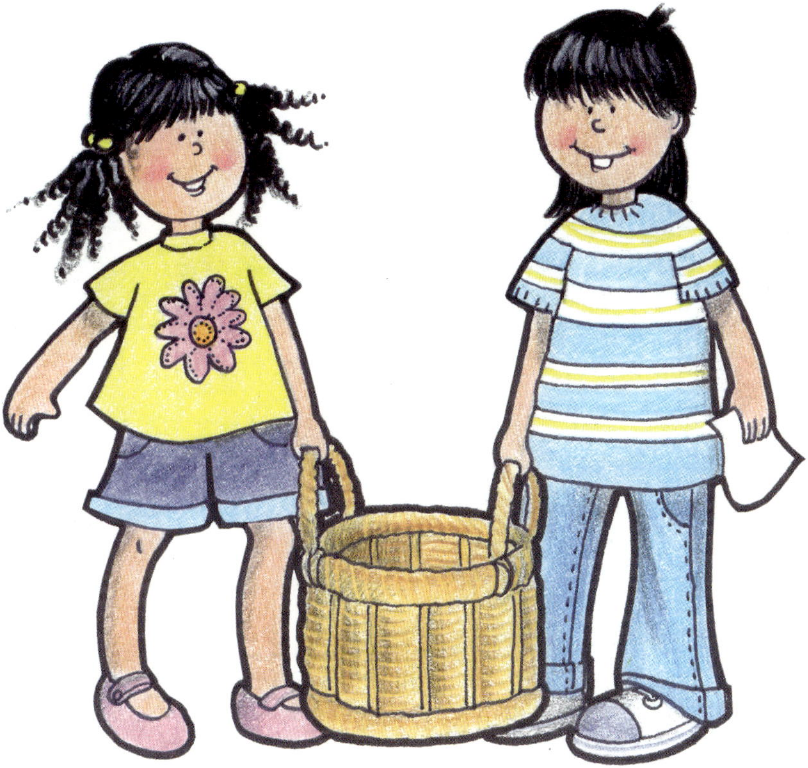

written by Pam Holden
illustrated by Pauline Whimp

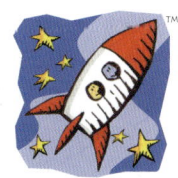

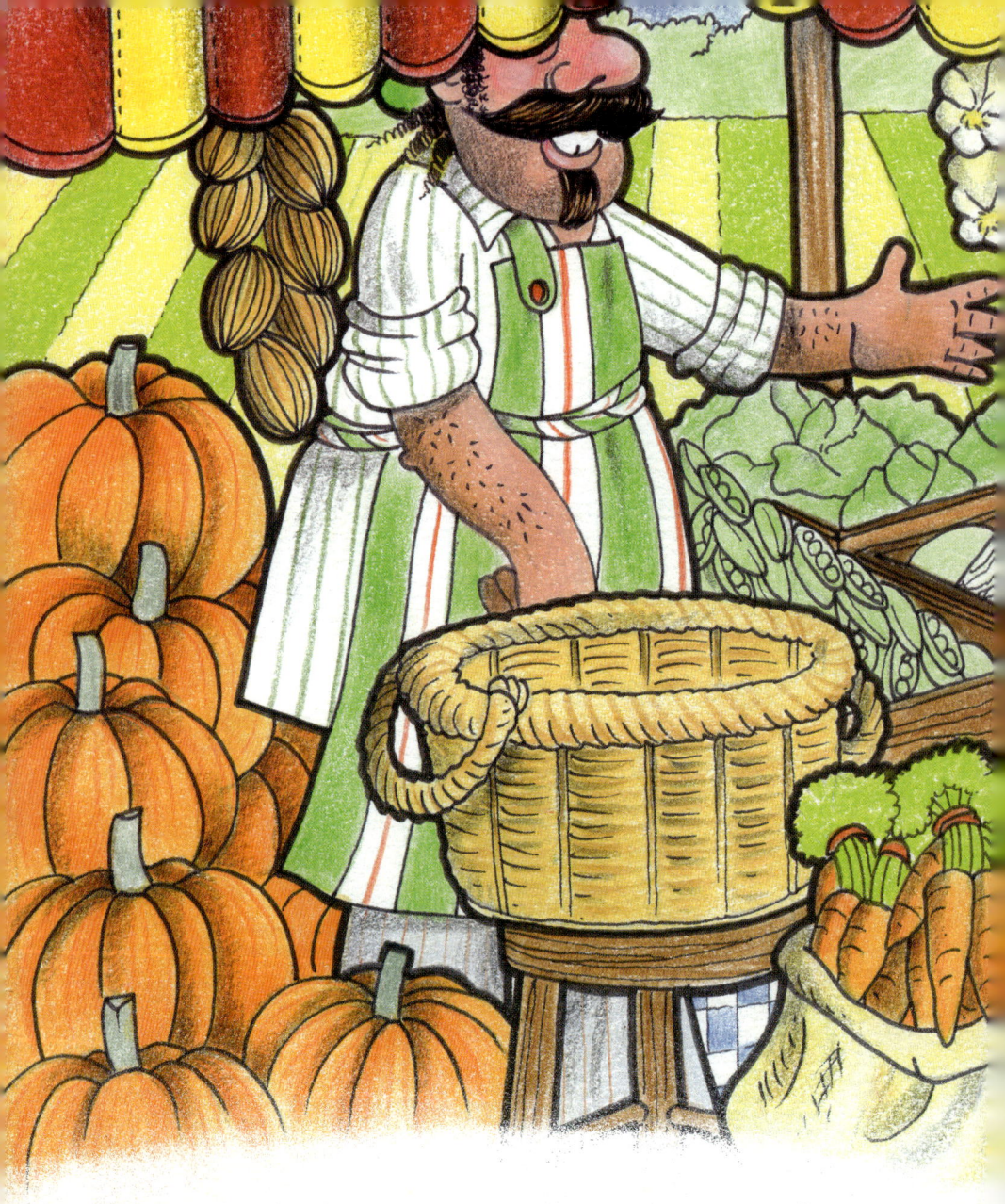

We like vegetables.

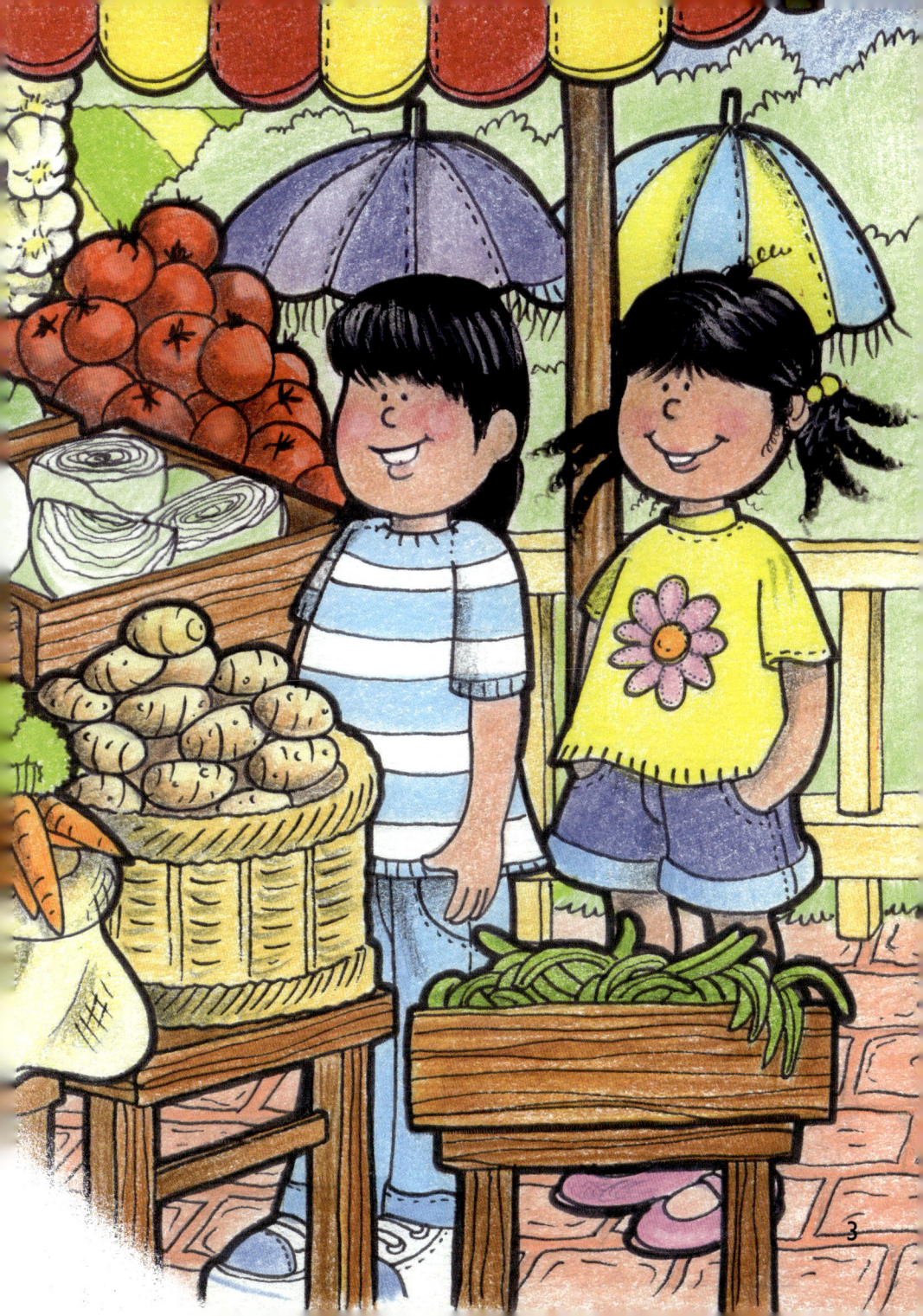

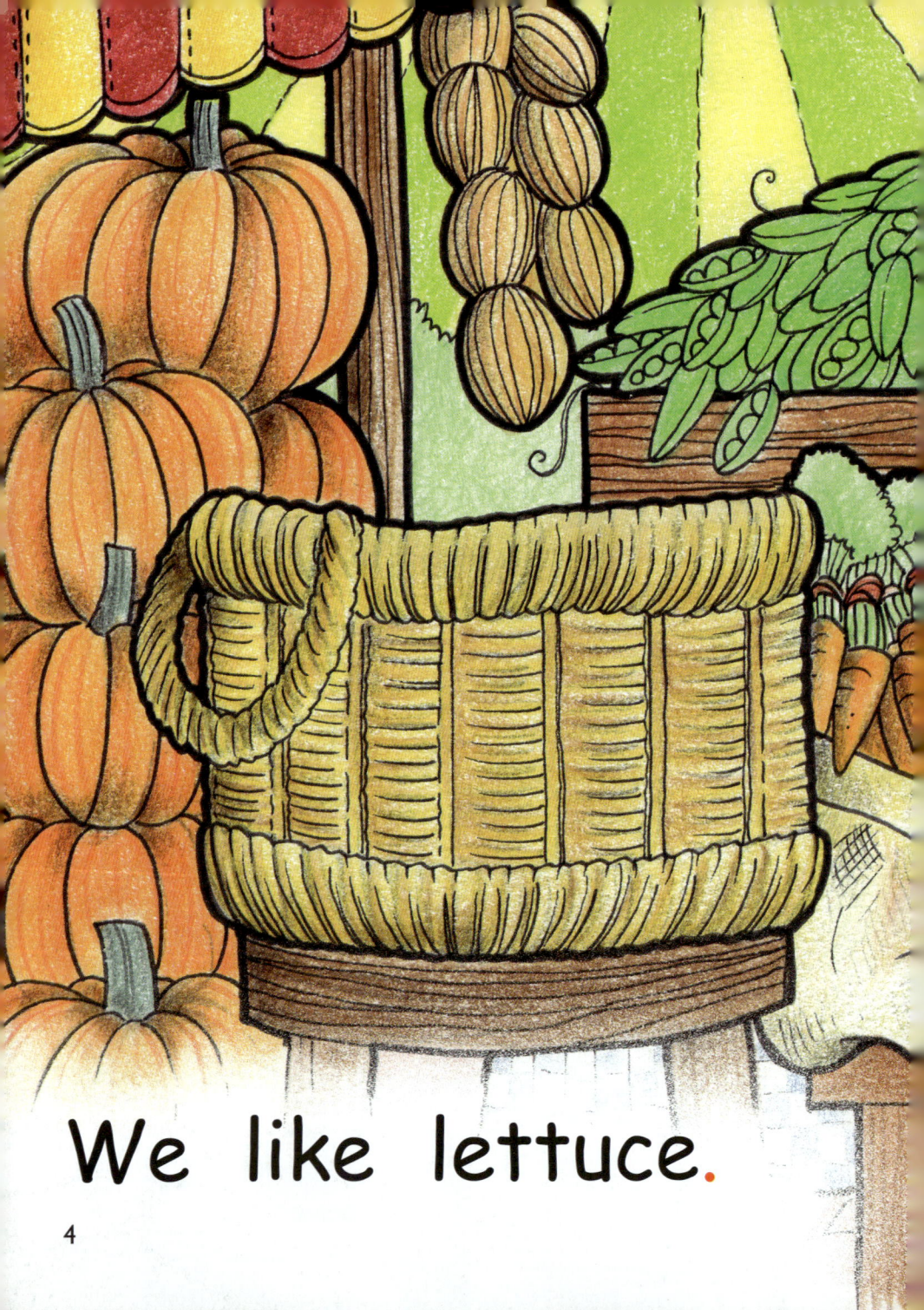
We like lettuce.

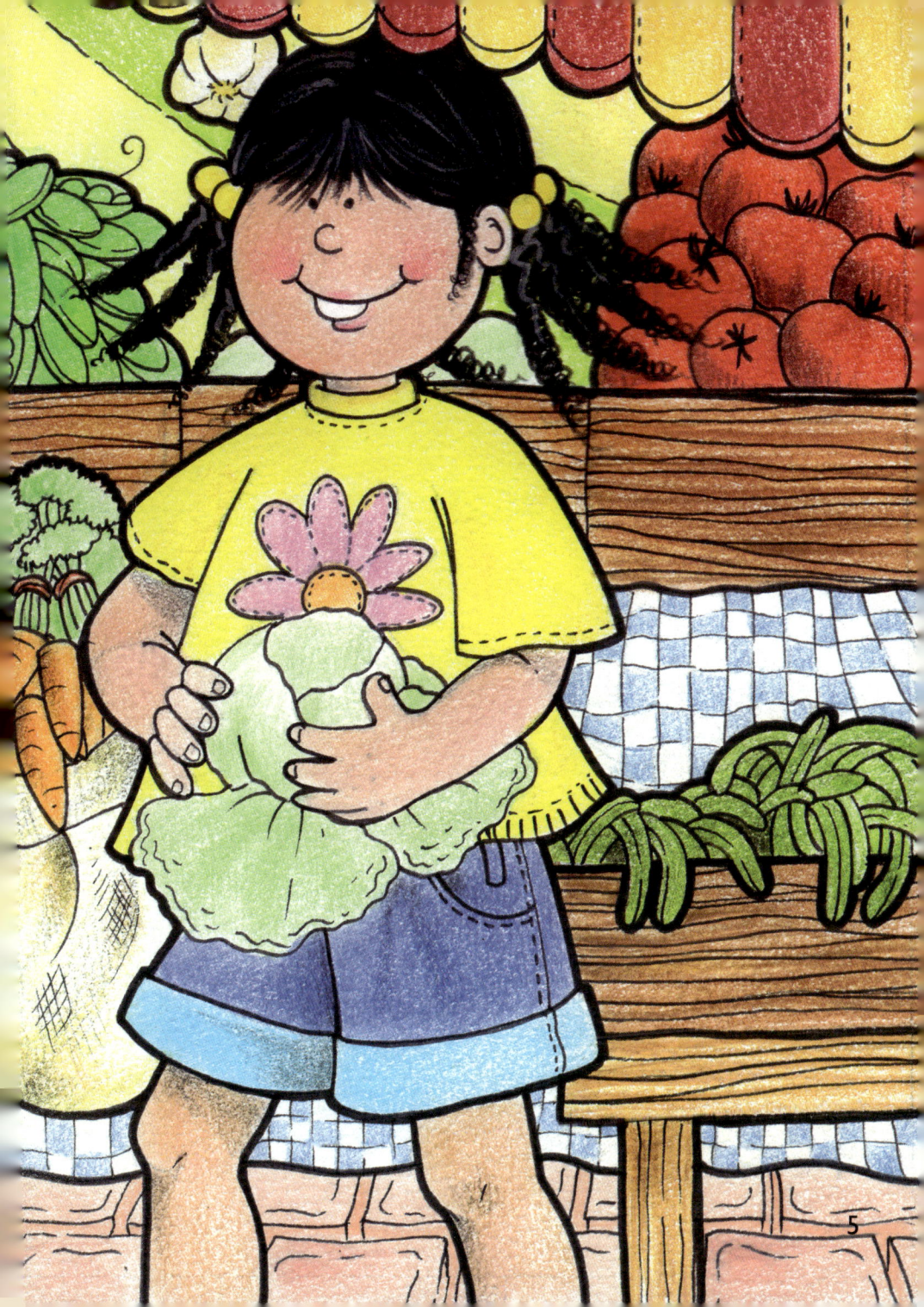

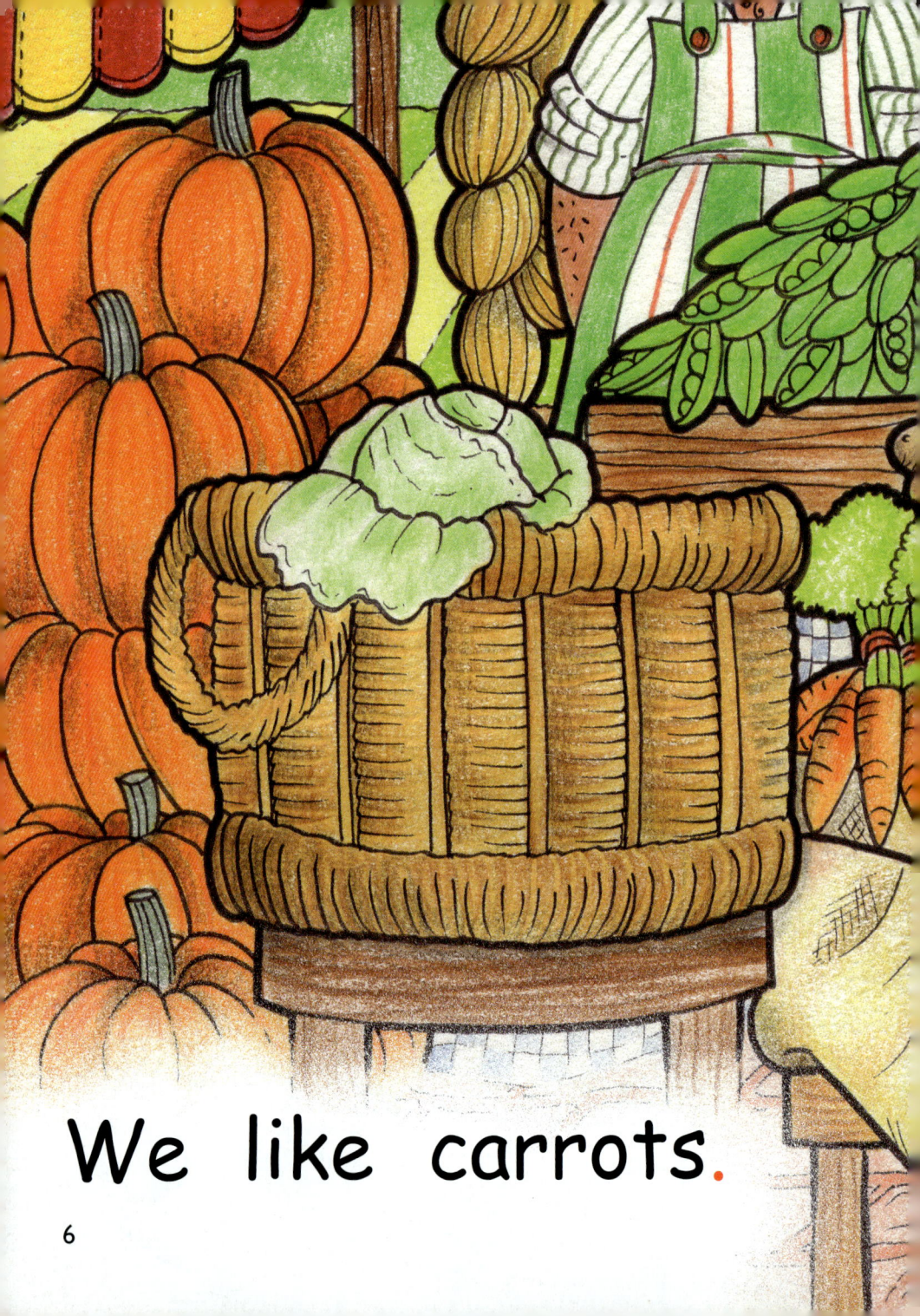

We like carrots.

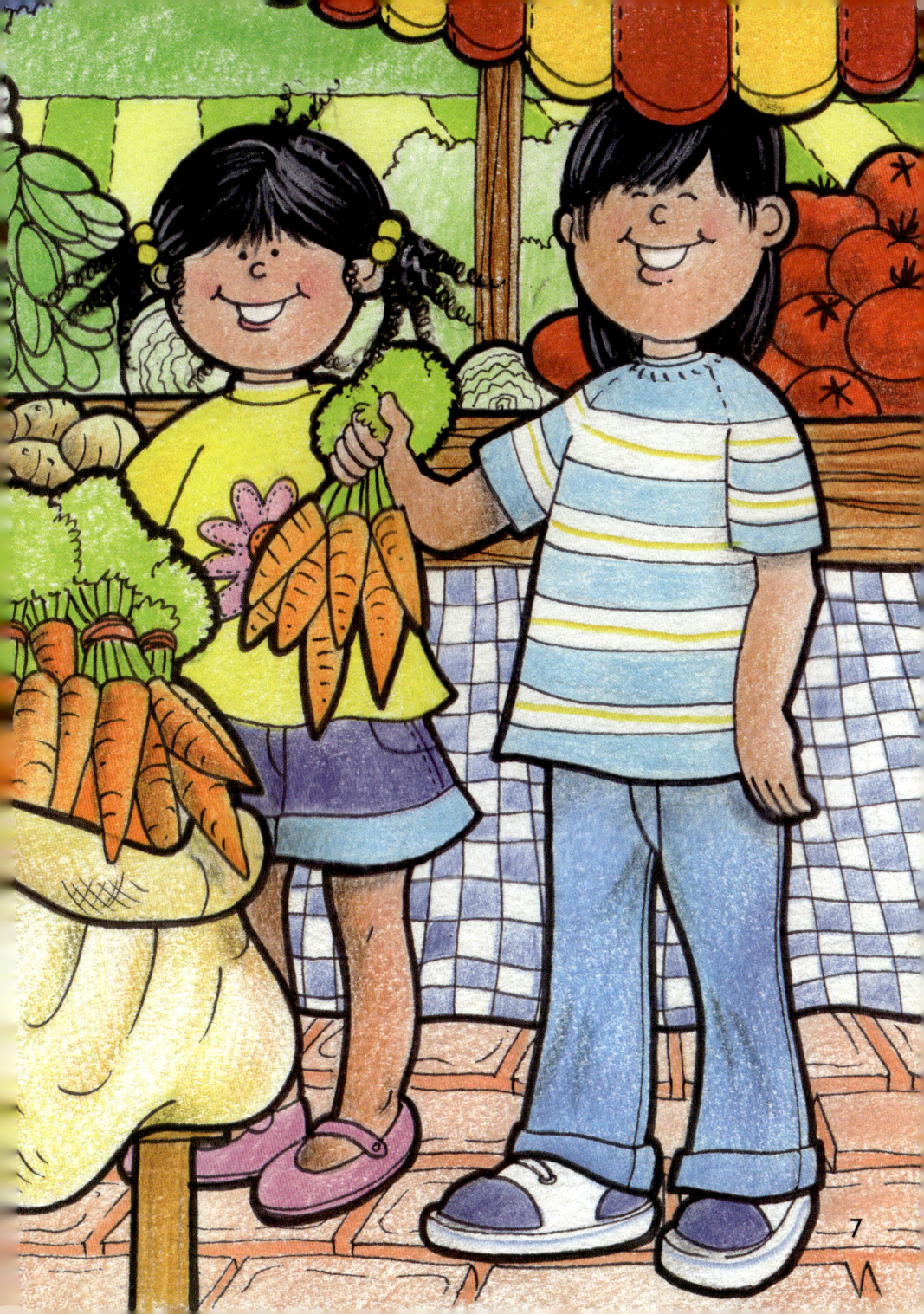

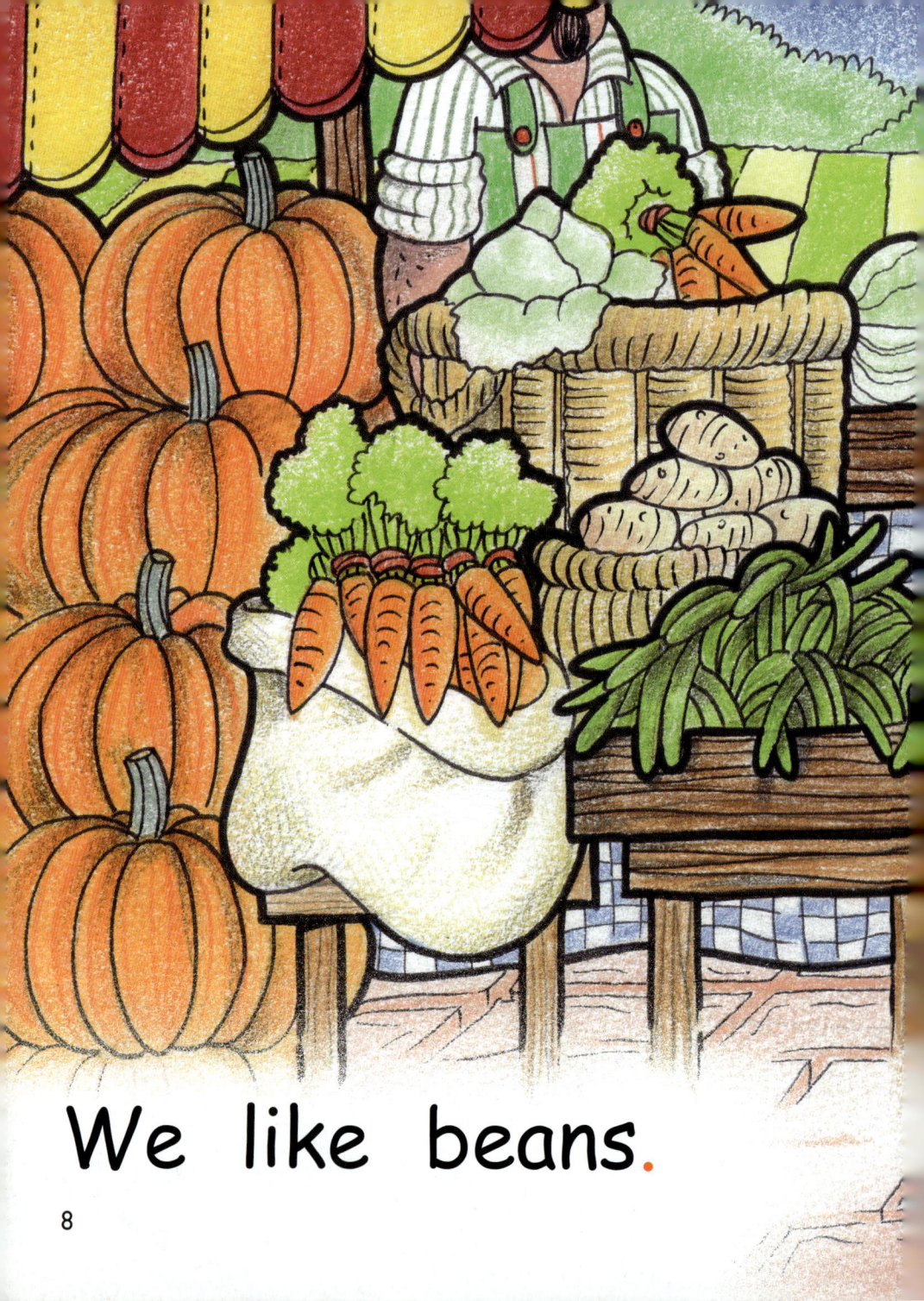

We like beans.

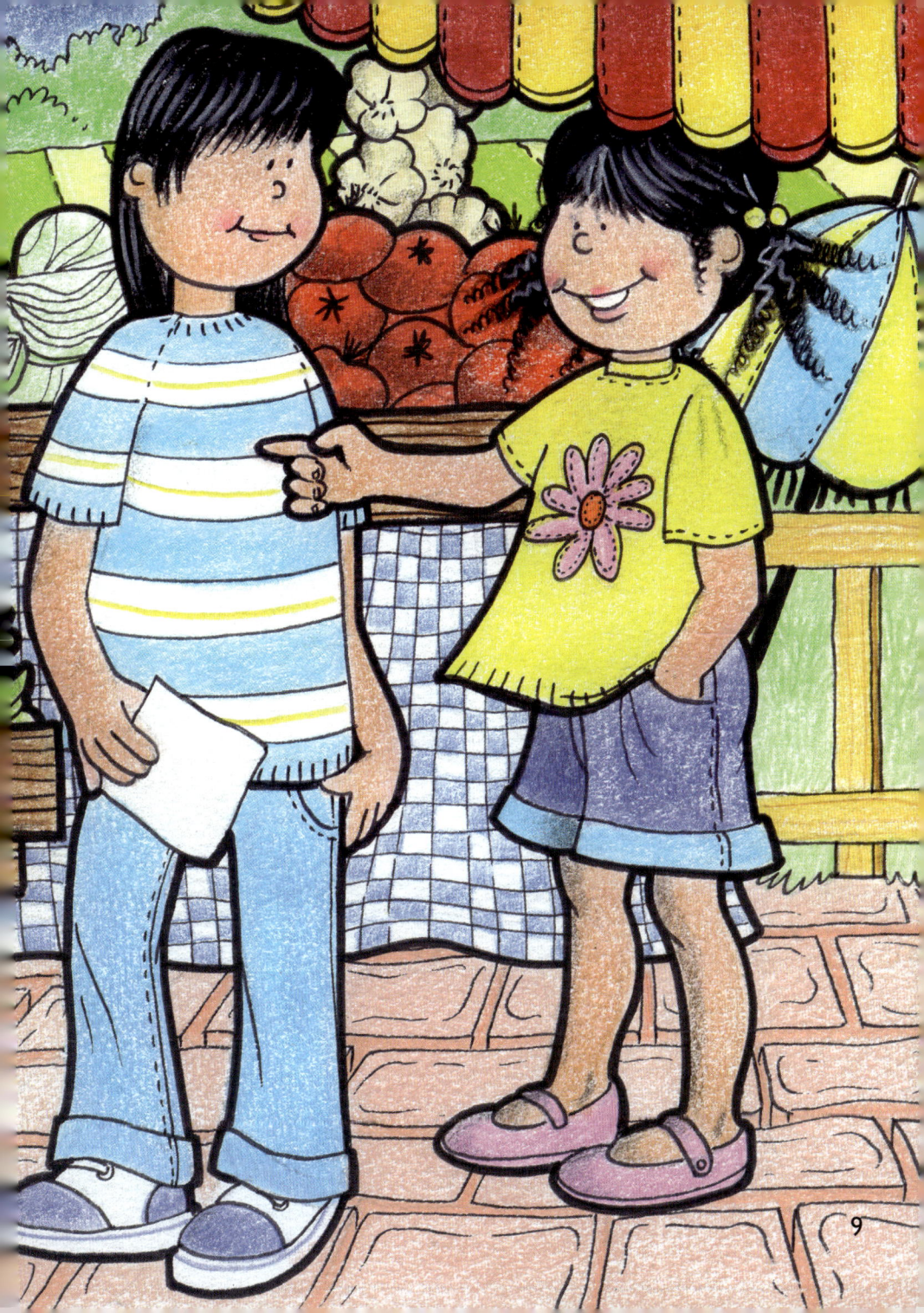

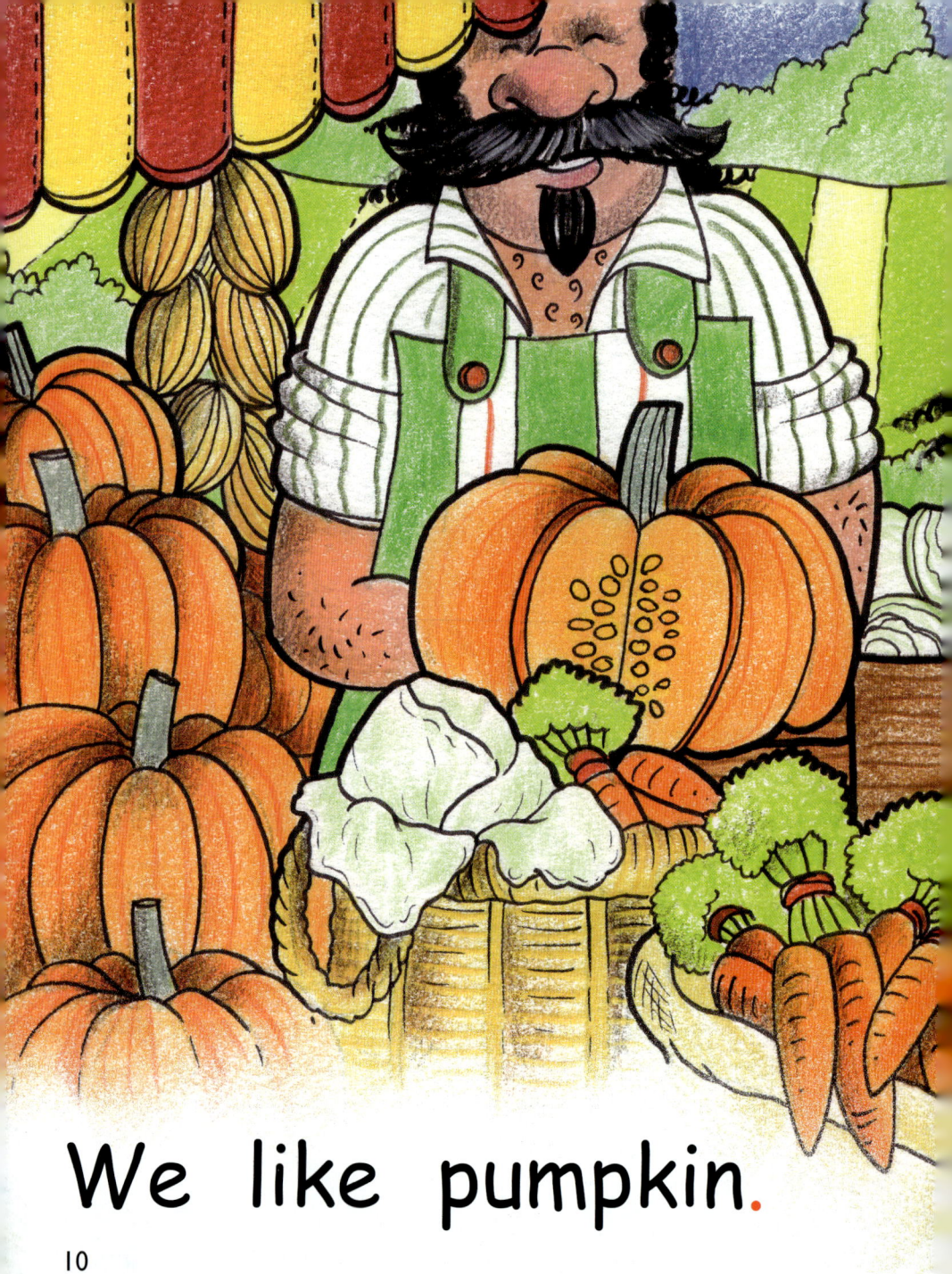

We like pumpkin.

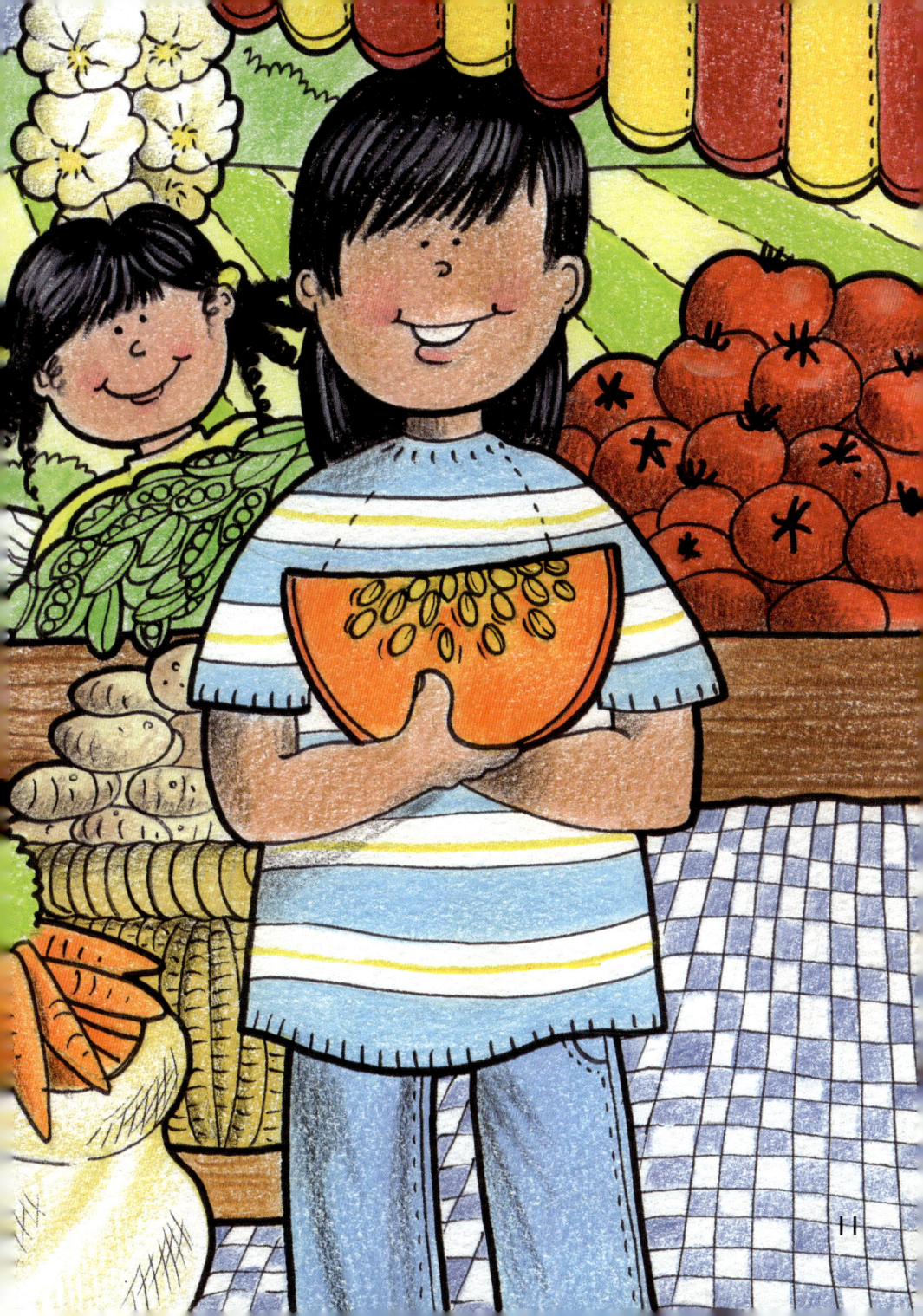

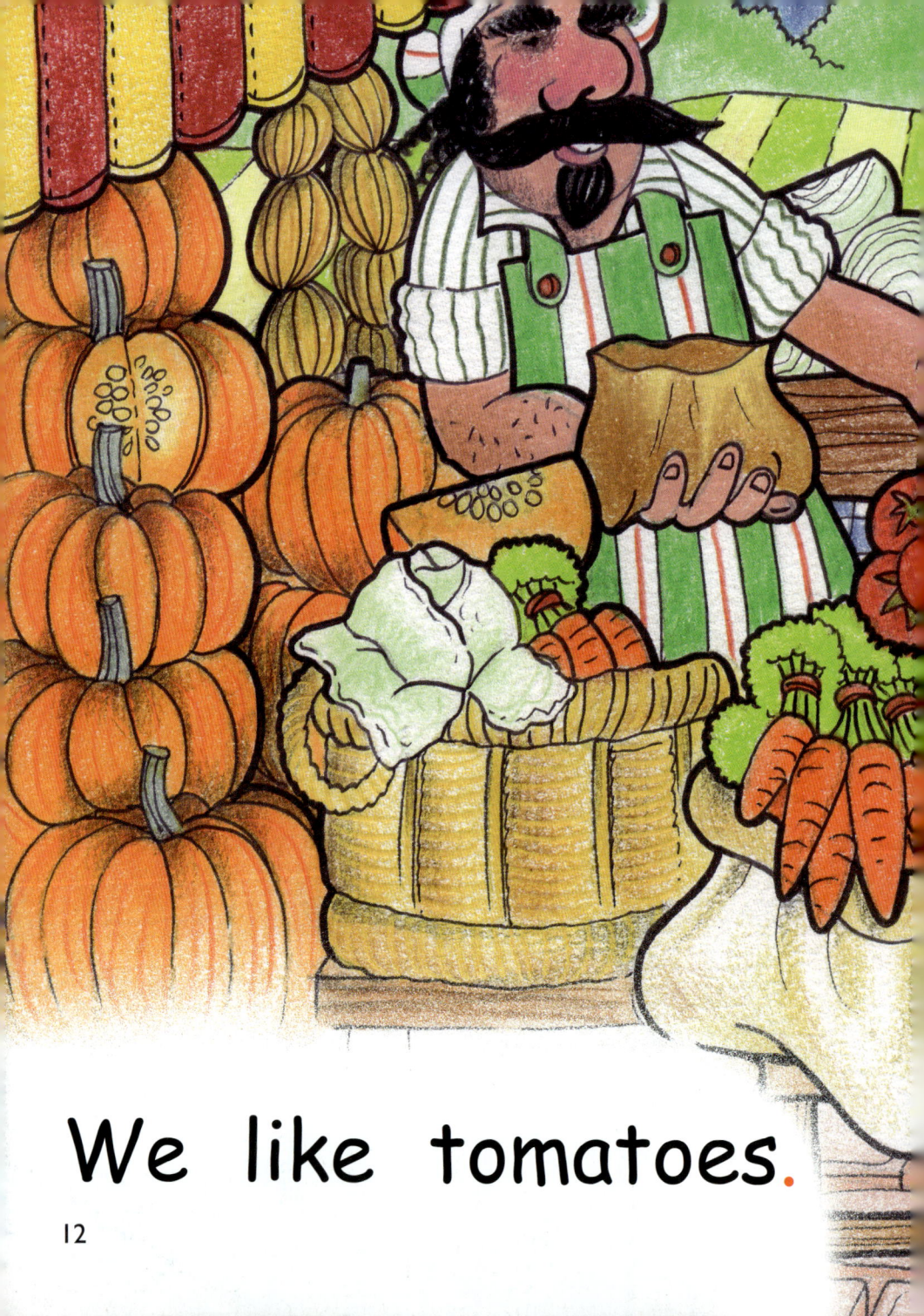

We like tomatoes.

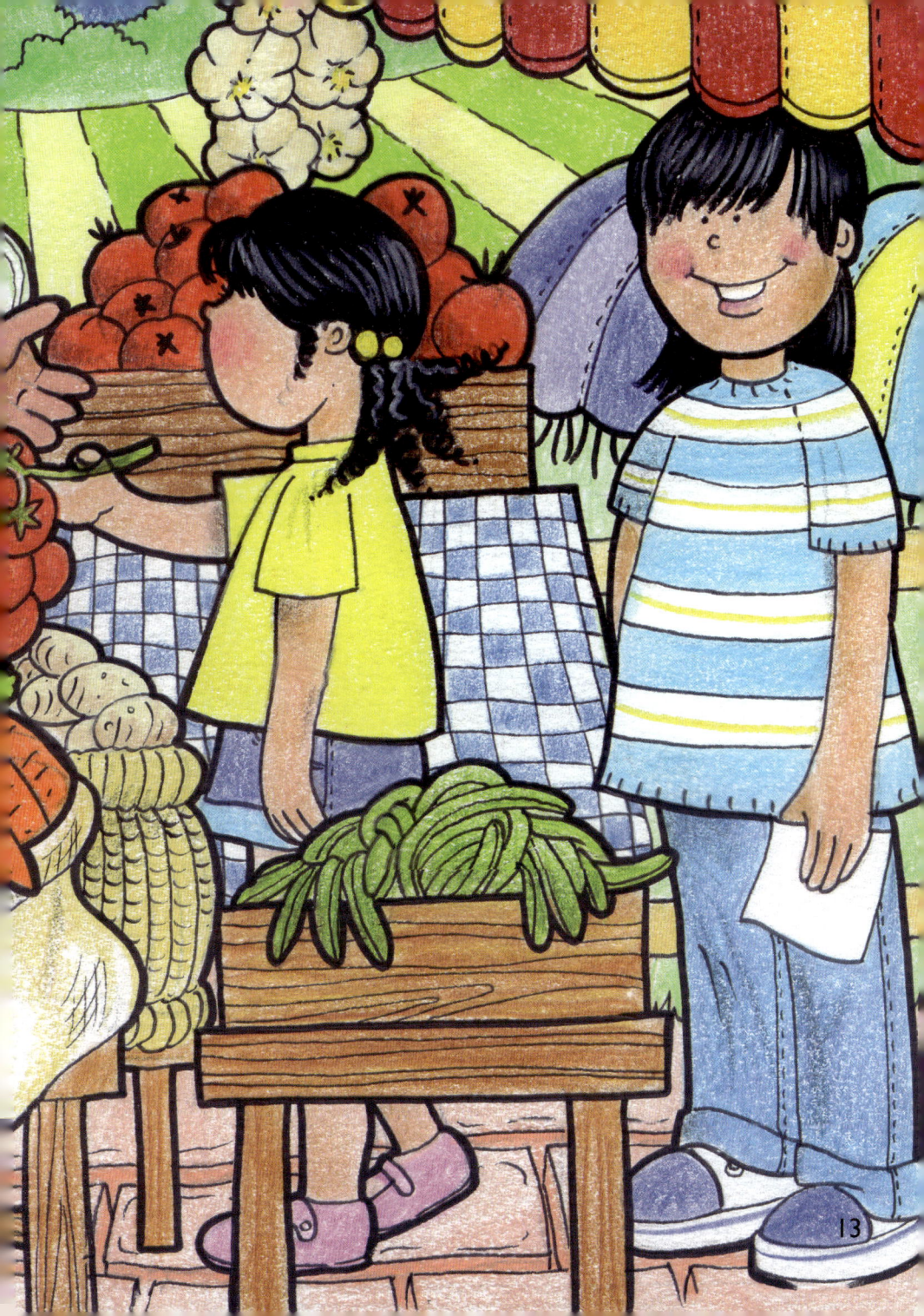

We like peas.

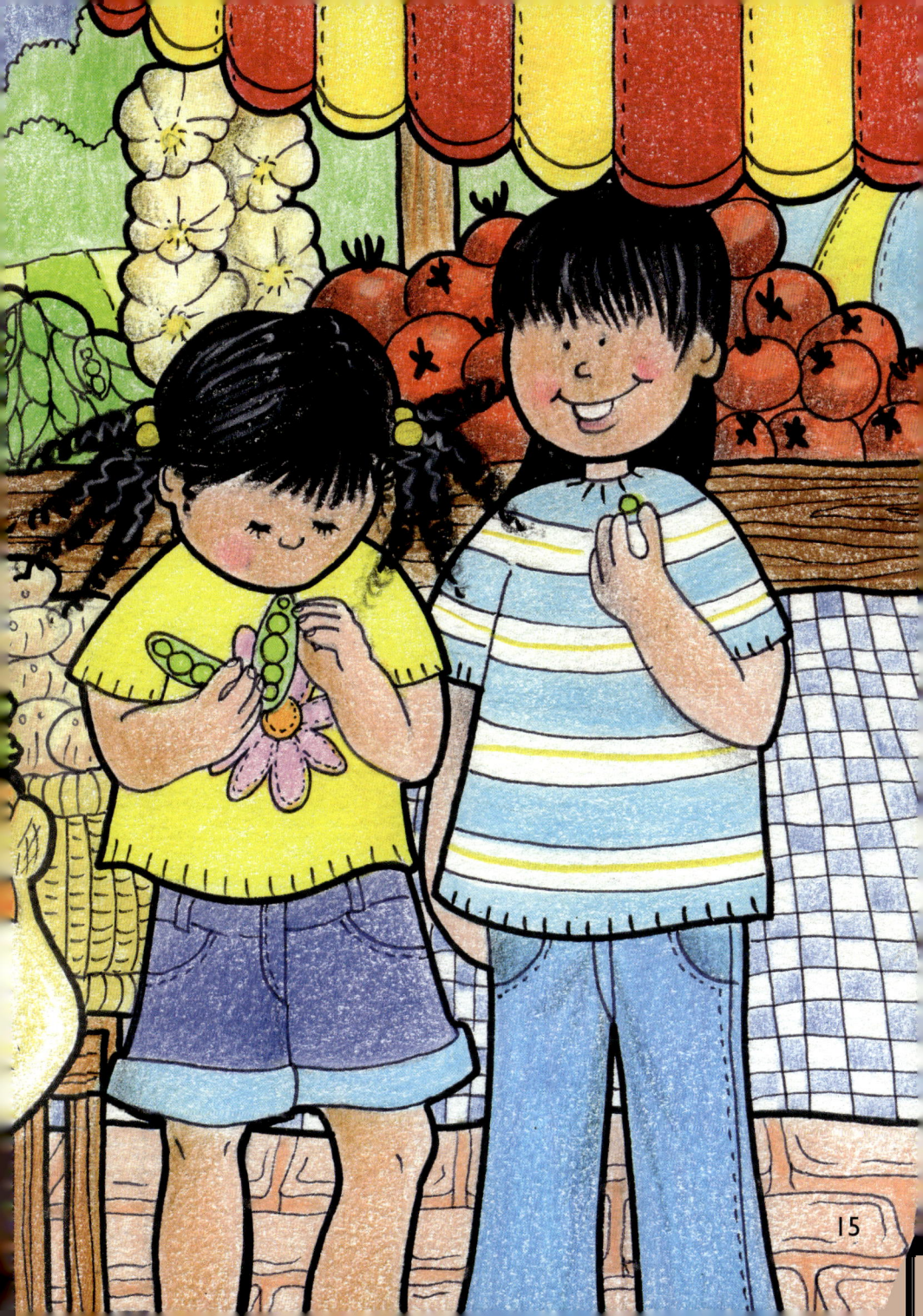

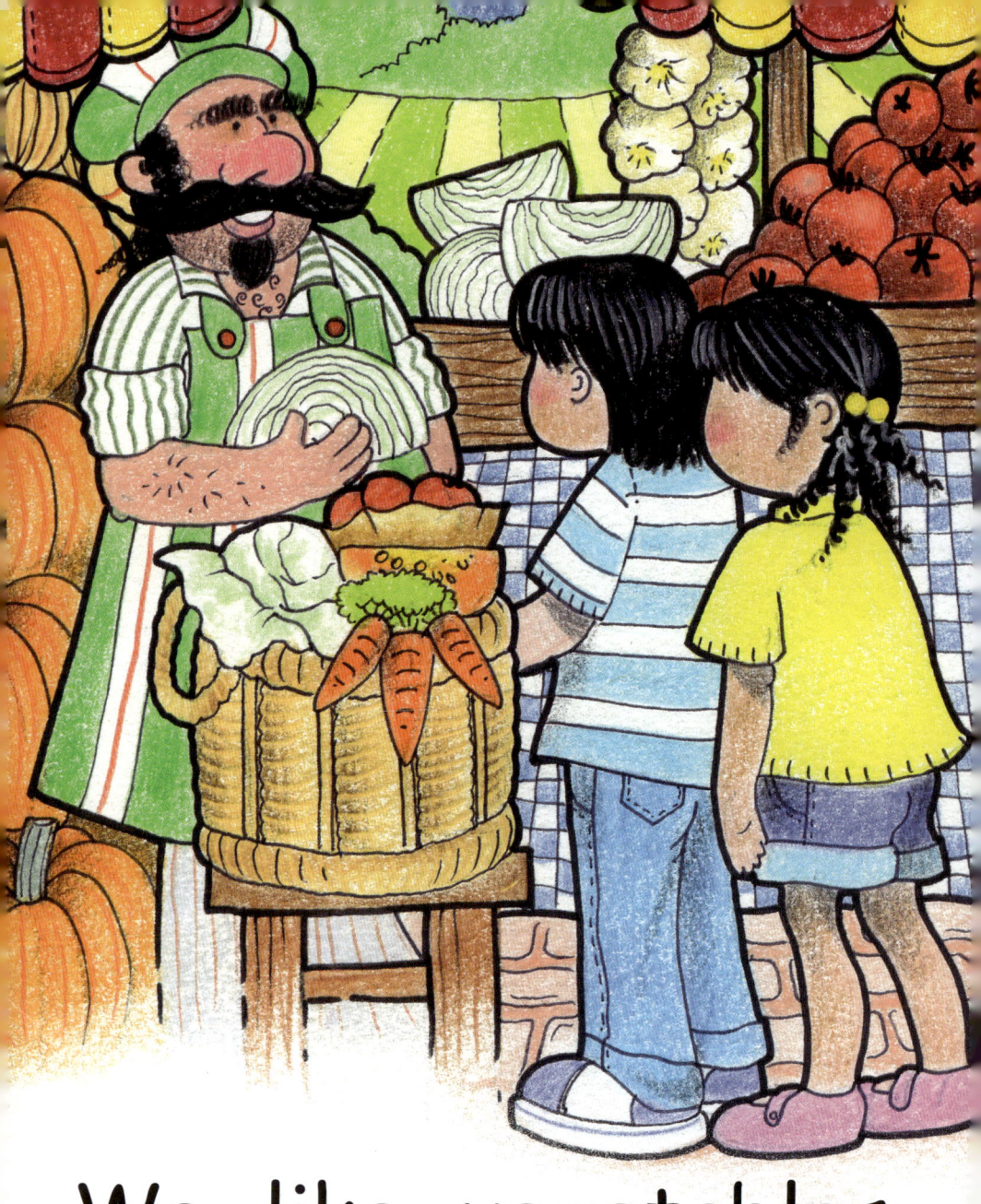

We like vegetables.